The Jungle Is My Home

The Jungle Is My Home

By Laura Fischetto · Illustrated by Letizia Galli

Viking

VIKING

Published by the Penguin Group

Viking Penguin, a division of Penguin Books USA Inc.,

375 Hudson Street, New York, New York 10014, U.S.A.

Penguin Books Ltd. 27 Wrights Lane, London W8 5TZ, England

Penguin Books Australia Ltd, Ringwood, Victoria, Australia

Penguin Books Canada Ltd, 2801 John Street, Markham, Ontario, Canada L3R 1B4

Penguin Books (N.Z.) Ltd, 182–190 Wairau Road, Auckland 10, New Zealand

Penguin Books Ltd, Registered Offices: Harmondsworth, Middlesex, England

First published in 1991 by Viking Penguin, a division of Penguin Books USA Inc.

1   3   5   7   9   10   8   6   4   2

Library of Congress Cataloging in Publication Data

Fischetto, Laura.

The jungle is my home / by Laura Fischetto ;

illustrated by Letizia Galli.   p.   cm.

Summary: Describes the jungle and how man's destructive behavior

threatens to ruin it as a unique home to a multitude of animals.

I S B N   0 - 6 7 0 - 8 3 5 5 0 - 1

1. Jungle ecology—Juvenile literature.   2. Deforestation—Environmental

aspects—Juvenile literature.   [1. Jungles.   2. Jungle animals.

3. Conservation of natural resources.]   I. Galli, Letizia, ill.   II. Title.

QH541.5.J8F57   1991   574.5′2642—dc20   90-24919   CIP   AC

Printed in Singapore   Set in 16 point Korinna

We and our beloved animals—
Cyrus, Potty, Topo, and Zar—
dedicate this book
to all the people and animals
who don't have enough love.

Letizia and Laura

There was a place
on earth where
it always rained but
you never got wet.
Where the trees
were very tall and
their branches made
a canopy. This place
was called a jungle.
Nobody seemed
to live in the jungle
but it was full of
beautiful noises.
And if you looked
closely you would see
that it was full
of houses and each
house was full
of busy animals.

Animals with long noses and long teeth lived on the
first floor of each house, where there was very little light.
These animals couldn't see further than the end of their
noses, so they didn't go out alone because they were afraid
they might bump into someone nasty.

They also knew it was not a good idea to get too friendly with the snakes because snakes have very wide mouths, and a nearsighted animal might wander inside by mistake and that would really be too bad.

Animals with long tails lived on the second floor. These animals were very absentminded. The minute they came into the house, they went out again and as soon as they were outside, they had to go back in because they had already forgotten what they had to do.

The animals with long arms lived on the third floor. These animals loved to be outside all the time. They liked to take everything they saw, hide everything they managed to take, and laugh when others complained.

The animals with long beaks and multicolored feathers lived in cool, luxurious penthouses high, high up on the top floors of the houses. They liked to sing a thousand songs.

The long-armed animals managed to climb up to the penthouses and they stole the loveliest feathers so they could wear them and look elegant.

The sloth was the one
among all these busy
animals who never
did a thing.

They all called him
Lazybones because he
just stayed in his
house and slept,
hanging upside down
by his long nails.

So he was asleep one
day when a man came
into the jungle.
The other animals ran
and hid because
they were frightened.

The man just drew a picture for his girlfriend on the animals' home.

Later, all the animals ran to look. They were curious because they did not know how to draw. Only Lazybones went on sleeping.

Very soon another man came. He wanted a piece of the animals' house because he had discovered that their homes made a nice fire which he could use for cooking and keeping warm. That time Lazybones woke up.

Lazybones went to look for a new home—very, very slowly, because he did not like walking. He did not know that another man was about to arrive.

Then his new house began to tremble and shake: it was about to fall!

The man took away
the animals' house
because he wanted
to use it to build
himself a canoe.
The long-nosed animals
and the long-tailed ones
and the ones with long
arms sadly gathered up
all their belongings
and went to look for
a new home.

But all the jungle
houses were already
full, so there was not
much room for the
homeless animals.

When they had all managed to settle into new homes, they noticed that Lazybones still had not arrived.

So the animals called and called for him. They had saved him a little spot since he only needed room to hang by his long nails and sleep.

Slowly, Lazybones reached the new house and they were all very glad to see him.

Then the long-nosed animals gathered food and helped their hosts clean the house.

The long-tailed animals kept on running into other long-tailed animals because the ones in the house wanted to go outside, and the outside ones wanted to go back in.

And the long-armed animals laughed because they loved confusion. The animals with the beautiful feathers were a bit rumpled because the upper floors were over-crowded, too.

The next time the men came they brought huge ma-
chines that made lots of noise. They did not want just one
house, but had come to get all the animals' houses.

One by one, the animals' houses tumbled
down and the animals had to run far, far away.

It is still raining on the silent, deserted jungle. A few animals stayed and are getting soaking wet because there are no more entwined branches to trap the rainwater.

Lazybones is alone. He does not know where to go and there is not a tree to hang from. He is waiting for someone to call him and tell him where to go.